SPUD GOES GREEN

the diary of my year as a greenie

Giles Thaxton, 29, lives on a big, old wooden boat in Wales. He is really quite green, but any further resemblance to Spud is purely coincidental. With a degree in Engineering, Design and Appropriate Technology from Warwick University he went on to work at the Centre for Alternative Technology in Mid-Wales. He now works as a carpenter in the same area. Giles plays the guitar in a band called Big Bunda and is into his black and white photography. This is his first book.

Nigel Baines When Nigel grew up in the 1970s waste was very much the order of the day. He remembers calculators the size of house bricks and televisions that would dim all the street lights when you switched them on. Now older and wiser and having seen retreating glaciers and endless traffic jams and streets full of plastic bags, Nigel is trying much harder to be more Spud-like. He even looks a little like him and wears a hat just like Spud's that he bought in Peru.

Giles Thaxton

SPUD GOES GREEN

Illustrated by
Nigel Baines

Spud's diary is printed on paper that is 100% recycled. We are trying to use recycled paper in all Egmont books. Where this is not possible we are making sure that our paper is not made from trees that have been chopped down illegally or come from ancient forests. Neither do we want paper made from fast-growing trees grown on land that used to be the home of ancient forest.

We want all of our paper to come from carefully managed forests that will live long into the future: for the creatures that live in them, the local people that rely on them and to make books for people like you.

EGMONT

We bring stories to life

First published 2006 by Egmont UK Limited
239 Kensington High Street, London W8 6SA
Text copyright © Egmont UK Limited
Illustrations copyright © Nigel Baines
The moral rights of the illustrator have been asserted
ISBN 1 4052 1731 6
1 3 5 7 9 10 8 6 4 2
Printed and bound in Singapore

Well, I've just bumped into Adi, my next-door neighbour, wearing a pair of swimming goggles. He's experimenting again. He says he wants to see how it will change his view of things. Apparently everything's gone green.

Adi said the colour suited me and suggested I should make it my New Year's Resolution to actually <u>turn</u> green. His idea is a good one, but I doubt my abilities to change colour. But I think I'll do the next best thing — I'll go green in a real friend-of-the-planet and looker-afterer-of-nature kind of way. From the sound of things, the planet needs someone else on its side.

Sunday 2nd January

I've thought hard about putting my New Year's Resolution plan into action and decided the best thing to do is to stay in bed all day. This way I won't do anything wrong that will harm the planet. Which is what being green is all about.

Monday 3rd January

I can stay in bed no longer. It's surprisingly tiring. I need advice on other ways to go green. I'll go next door — Adi knows a lot about a lot of things. He'll know what's green and what's not. And what's what.

Well, Adi is dead impressed with my green plan and has come up with my first eco challenge.

The Heat Leak Hunt

I have to find every single heat leak spot in the house. I can do that. Easy. You see, I have a highly sophisticated plan:

1. I have found a length of lightweight ribbon about half as long as my arm and I've tied it to the end of a pencil.

2. And now I'm going round the house to watch it wiggle ... A wiggling ribbon tells me that there is a draught, which means there's a gap, which means I need to plug it.

3. The detective work continues ... A right lot of wiggling going on now. Whoops. Better shut the kitchen window. Still a bit draughty though. Another heat leak?

Adi says a dedicated greenie like me needs to make sure that heat doesn't leak out through gaps under the doors or around the windows. That's how it gets wasted.

Tuesday 4th January

Well, having located all the heat leak trouble spots I now need to do something about them. And I think I know how ... I've found some old clothes and have been cutting them up and sewing them into a tube. Make way for the first sausage snake! Perfect for stopping the draught under the door.
This going green malarkey is easy ...

'Run for it, Spud! I'll hold him as long as I can. The venom is surely **DEADLY.**'

(Adi got a shock though. It took me a long while and reasoned argument to convince him he wasn't actually in danger.)

BREED YOUR OWN SNAKE

1. Cut a piece of material into a rectangle about as long as the width of a door and about half as wide.

2. Fold the cloth in two along its length.

3. Sew all along the length and the two ends of the cloth, leaving a small opening to turn it inside out.

4. Then turn it inside out, to hide the seam.

5. Stuff your snake with newspaper and scraps of cloth, right down to the end.

6. Sew up the opening and paint on some eyes. Easy peasy!

WARNING! Be careful with all things sharp, like scissors and needles. Get a grown-up to face the danger instead of you.

Wednesday 5th January

Today perhaps I should see whether I can survive with the heating turned off altogether? I'll save loads of electricity!

1 p.m. I'm freezing. I've squeezed on a couple of extra jumpers. Maybe this isn't such a good idea. Hang on, someone at the door.

Adi! Trapped outside! My front door was frozen shut. I had to explain the situation through the letterbox: the door needed a good shove. 'Right,' I said. 'When I nod my head, you hit it.' Adi said he didn't see how hitting my head would help. When we eventually got the door open a blast of wind whooshed into the kitchen — it was warmer outside than in.

Adi says I should put the heating back on, but not as high as before, and wear a jumper. His wise words always impress me.

Monday 10th January

Right. Well, I've just gone a-visiting and found Adi on the floor, staring at his bin! He said he was worried. According to him, all our rubbish ends up in a hole called a landfill site, where it breaks down, giving off smelly gases and polluting the air. (Bit like Adi after a big meal.) But as if that isn't bad enough, some things don't rot down for thousands of years, like plastic, glass and metal, and just pile up and up ... Adi and I have discussed it at length and decided the best thing to do is to create less rubbish in the first place. It's going to be tricky.

Adi assures me if you shout continuously at a cup of water for eight years you produce enough sound energy to heat it.

FACT FOR THE DAY

ooo Never mind about MY feelings

Adi tells me we can pick out
some rubbish and rebicycle it,
including:

Glass jars and bottles

Plastic bottles

Drinks cans

**Tin cans, like baked
beans tins**

(I'm going to stack this lot at the side
of the stairs.) **Paper and cardboard – which I will have to
pack upstairs, in the little room.**

**Clothes. Like that purple
jumper I never wear.**

But what then? I don't see what this has
got to do with bikes, or landfill sites.

Monday 17th January

I've been collecting stuff to rebicycle for a week now. There's not an inch to move. The baked beans tin from lunch was the last straw — it started a mini landslide down the stairs. When can I start rebicycling?

It turns out Adi said <u>recycling</u>. I wondered what bikes had to do with it. It seems all these containers I've been collecting can be melted down to make new ones. Very clever.

Adi pounced on that purple jumper and has been wearing it ever since. Apparently that's also called recycling.

Thursday 3rd February

In the end Adi and I had to make four trips to the recycling centre with our rubbish collections! I'm pooped. Adi says I could make it easier on myself by creating less rubbish in the first place. Bit tricky, but a good thing to try and do. Adi's been keeping his rubbish in his pockets. But where from, there? He says he hasn't got to that stage yet. (Big pockets.) From now on I will be making a few greenie changes to the way I do things though ...

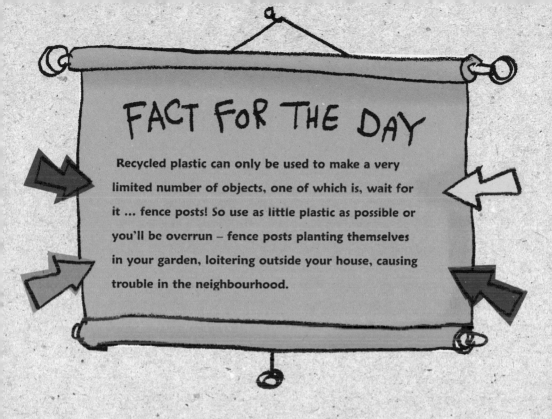

FACT FOR THE DAY

Recycled plastic can only be used to make a very limited number of objects, one of which is, wait for it ... fence posts! So use as little plastic as possible or you'll be overrun – fence posts planting themselves in your garden, loitering outside your house, causing trouble in the neighbourhood.

1. I've been refilling an old bottle instead of buying a new one every time I need a drink of water or juice.

2. I'm drinking fewer canned drinks.

3. I'm not going to buy food wrapped up in lots of plastic packaging unless there's nothing else and I'm really hungry.

Wednesday 9th February

I've been watching this bird all morning. (I think it's a sparrow.) He has been hanging around outside the kitchen window, pacing back and forth. Perhaps he needs somewhere to sit? I have poked around in the shed and found some lengths of wood to make a bird table.

1. You need a long, thin, straight piece of wood at least 130 cm long. This will be the stand.

2. Find a square piece of wood to make the tabletop. It should be at least the size of this book. But don't use this book.

3. This is tricky so you might as well get someone older to do it for you. They need to screw the tabletop on to the end of the stick.

4. Decide where you want your bird table to go, dig a hole and stick the post in.

5. Fill around the post with soil and stamp it down solid.

Adi says birds have a tough time these days. Trees and hedgerows are cut down to make room for roads and houses, so they are running out of places to live. What they need is more bird tables — somewhere for them to have a stop and a think and a munch on a berry or two. Just what we all need.

Sunday 13th February

The birds have been flocking round that bird table like it is the hip and happening place to be. And covering it with bird poo. A very good sign. They obviously like the food I have been putting out:

Breadcrumbs from wholemeal bread

Fat – left over from my fried breakfast

Nuts

Dried fruit

Cheese

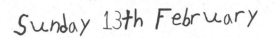

Adi says DON'T give them:

Salted peanuts

Pieces of white bread

Desiccated coconut

Uncooked meat – I can see why.

Spicy food – this I don't understand. They are missing out.

Reserved

Adi and I have concluded
that I am well on the way to becoming
really quite green. Long gone are the days
of not at all green or only a little bit green.
I'm not yet truly green, I admit. But I am
going to keep working at it.

FACT FOR THE DAY

**Reusing rubbish is even greener than
recycling it. So I get extra bonus points for
my bird table! Adi says he is monitoring my
progress and keeping a strict score card.**

Friday 18th February

This afternoon I was watching the gang at the bird table when it came to me. Those birds need somewhere to sleep and lay eggs. What about a hotel? And I could make it from something I would normally throw away, like a cardboard milk carton. How green would that be? I think I'm a natural.

1. One milk carton from my recycling pile.

2. I'll open out the top and give the carton a wash.

3. A round hole in the front with some scissors – about the size of a bath plug. The grand entrance. (DANGER! Spiky scissors.)

4. Some dry grass inside to make it warm and comfy for the guests.

5. Close up the top and seal it with some parcel tape.

6. Out come the paints – it has to look good so that the birds want to go inside.

7. Over the door I'm going to write 'Bird hotel – enjoy your stay'. Then I'll dangle it from a tree in the garden with some string.

Now I just have to wait for the first customers. If I made more bird hotels from recycled milk cartons there would be far less rubbish to worry about and hundreds of happy birds. Good plan.

Saturday 19th February

Adi and I have been digging a pond. The idea is to attract more wildlife into the garden. Snails and dragonflies will love it. So will frogs and toads, and they make great burping noises. We have a lot in common. I'll get fish too — loads of them. It will be humming with activity by the time we've finished.

So, that's what Adi and I have been up to this afternoon. Talking and digging. Digging and talking. Him talking. Me digging.

This is how The Great Pond got built:
(Very tricky so don't do it on your own.)

1. We dug a hole. A big hole. One side is a shallow slope so if anything falls in it can crawl out again. Including me.

2. We lined it with bits of old carpet to cover up any sharp stones.

3. Then we laid a piece of thick plastic on top. This will stop the water draining away. We put some big stones around the edge to hold the plastic down and mark out the edge. Next time it rains the pond should start filling up.

Now we wait for rain. Adi and I have been admiring our handiwork. He says if we had dug a bigger hole we could have cut it in half and Adi could have put the other half in his garden.
Good green progress today.

Sunday 20th February

It rained cats and dogs last night. The garden is full of poodles! Ba boom. And I've just had a look at the pond: it's started filling up. Another couple of nights like that and we'll be nearly there.

Adi says the next thing to do is to buy special pond plants. There are three types:

1. Oxygenating plants: put oxygen into the water, which fish and any other pond-life need to breathe. These plants grow entirely underwater and give fish somewhere to hide if they're feeling shy.

2. Floating plants: most of these are rooted at the bottom of the pond. Their leaves float on the surface, creating shade, which is important to a lot of pond-life.

3. Marginal plants: these usually have flowers, which produce nectar, which attracts bees and other wildlife.

TIP FOR THE DAY

If you float a ball on the surface of your pond in the winter it will stop the water freezing over and will let oxygen in so that the plants and fish can breathe.

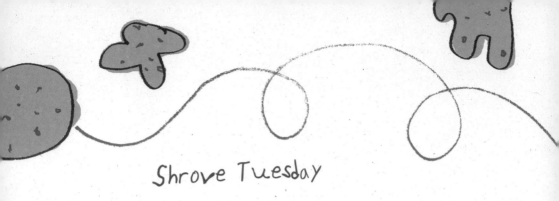

Shrove Tuesday

Shrove Tuesday means it's Pancake Day!
And a kitchen and an Adi on Pancake Day is a
dangerous combination. Adi was confident he
could flip them, but I was right to be sceptical.

It's a well known fact — you
can dodge falling pancakes
successfully for only so
long. And pulling soggy
pancake out of your hair
is not easy.

I've been thinking. Adi says that the lorries, ships and planes that transport our food to the shops use up gallons of fuel, and pour out stinky fumes that pollute the air. So really I should be trying to get food from closer to home. There's no closer than my own back garden. So I'm thinking I could grow my own food ...

Sunday 6th March

Adi thinks I should go for it and get growing — or stop eating altogether. That seems a little drastic. The first thing I need to do is to collect seeds.

Adi left an apple core on the kitchen table — messy guy. I was just about to give it to the birds when I twigged: the pips are seeds. Adi left it there on purpose. I'll keep them and plant them. When I'm older I'll have an orchard where the garden used to be. I'll have apples coming out of my ears.

1. Pips from old varieties of fruits like Cox's apples are best for planting up as they have better genes. (Genes are the information inside the pips that show them how to grow. Not to be mixed up with the things that keep your legs warm.)

2. An apple a day keeps the doctor away. If you aim correctly.

APPLE FACTS FOR THE DAY

Sunday 13th March

I have been collecting up pots all week so that I can plant those apple pips and a few other seeds I have saved — avocado, grape, tomato ... There are yoghurt pots, plastic tubs and cleaned-out paint tins all round the house. I'm going to try using an old trainer as well. Any plant in there will probably die of suffocation, but we'll see. I'll start with the tomato seeds... and perhaps those apple pips. I don't know if this will work, but hey, it's worth a shot. And Adi seems convinced ...

TOMATOES!

Adi tells me my best bet is to save seeds from a locally grown tomato. These seeds are ready to grow straightaway. Seeds from supermarket tomatoes need help to improve their chances ...

1. Scoop out the tomato seeds together with the insides and put it all in a bowl.

2. Leave the bowl in a warm place for a few days so that the seeds ferment. Little bubbles will appear and it will start to smell a bit.

3. Then rinse the seeds in a strainer under running water and leave them out on a small plate to dry.

4. Put them in the fridge for a few days. This will trick them! The seeds will think they are outside and it is frosty winter time so when you take them out, they assume it must be spring – when seeds start growing. Crafty, hey?

Sunday 20th March

Now's the right time of year for planting apple and tomato seeds, so this morning ... .

1. I used a screwdriver to punch a hole through the base of all those pots I collected. This is so the water can drain out. (Watch out! Danger! Danger! Make sure you get someone to do this for you – it's not easy.)

2. I put a few little stones at the bottom of each pot to stop the soil falling out and to help the water drain away. Plants don't like their roots sitting in water.

3. Each pot was filled with soil, nearly up to the top.

4. Then I gently pressed a few apple pips into some, and a few tomato seeds into others, all a fingerwidth apart. Some of the seeds won't germinate, so if there are a few in each then chances are at least one of them will grow.

5. I covered them over with a little more soil so the seeds were about a centimetre under the surface. Then I watered them.

Each pot is now sitting on the kitchen window sill, where it is bright but not too warm. I had to put the trainer by the back door, for obvious reasons. Hope those little tomato seeds will be OK in there. I don't fancy their chances.

Friday 1st April

It's April Fool's Day — one of the best days of the year. I was setting up a fantastic practical joke involving a bucket of cold water balanced on a branch with a length of rope running all the way from the bucket handle to the front door knob, when the phone rang. It was Adi. He sounded very excited and gasped 'Come over quick' before hanging up.

I raced over and found him staring at a pot on the kitchen table. It was a little tree — with coins hanging from the branches!

'A money tree,' Adi babbled. 'I planted some coins in a fit of experimentation and this is what grew.' I was astounded. Adi carefully picked off a coin and placed it in my hand. 'Plant this, Spud,' he said. 'You will be a rich man.'

This was fantastic. I ran home, flung open the front door and only just caught sight of a bucket tipping, water falling.

Now I'm not even so sure about this coin. The cold bucket shower has brought me to my senses.

Sunday 3rd April

Easter Sunday! Today I hid ten Easter eggs around the garden, counting them out carefully, and Adi hid ten for me in his. He arrived back later with fourteen. Seemed a bit strange, but then I checked my secret personal supply. Not secret enough. So eating chocolate is what I've been up to this afternoon. All our eggs were wrapped in only a little plastic and cardboard so there's less to recycle. I feel very green and pleased with myself. And sick. I've checked to see if there's any life showing in my plant pots. And there isn't. Early days though.

Tuesday 5th April

My plants are going to need a fair amount of water. A stroke of luck — I found a bucket I thought I had lost full to the brim with rainwater.

Catching rainwater for plants is a top idea, because it saves using too much water from the taps. And that is important because:

1. Only a tiny part of the world's water is fresh water — about 1%. The rest is seawater, which is far too salty to drink. And 99% of the fresh water is locked up in the Polar ice caps. So that means that there is not much water to go around if you think how much water everyone uses for washing, drinking, cooking and shooting with water pistols. Especially a fine, big water pistol. With which I plan to get Adi when he least expects it.

Polar ice caps

2. Even in parts of the world where it rains quite often there are only a limited number of places to store the water for dry periods when the sun is out and there is no rain at all.

3. The weather is quite unpredictable these days: hot summers with very little rain in some parts of the world, and rainstorms and flooding in others. It is difficult to predict just what will happen in the future. So for the time being it is a good idea to get in the habit of being careful how much water you use.

4. A third of all the water we produce is ... flushed down the loo!

Adi says he has been collecting rainwater. When it rains the water runs off his roof, along the gutter, through the down-pipe, and straight into a big barrel. He doesn't drink the water, but the plants love it and when it gets too hot he jumps in to cool down!

FACT FOR THE DAY

A leaky tap wastes up to half a million pints of water a year. Time for a plumber ... I'm going to stop leaving the tap running when I brush my teeth. That will save water too.

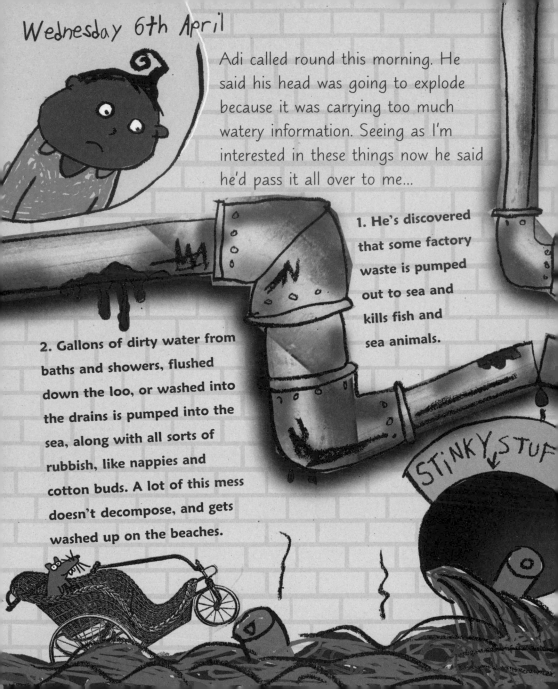

Wednesday 6th April

Adi called round this morning. He said his head was going to explode because it was carrying too much watery information. Seeing as I'm interested in these things now he said he'd pass it all over to me...

1. He's discovered that some factory waste is pumped out to sea and kills fish and sea animals.

2. Gallons of dirty water from baths and showers, flushed down the loo, or washed into the drains is pumped into the sea, along with all sorts of rubbish, like nappies and cotton buds. A lot of this mess doesn't decompose, and gets washed up on the beaches.

STINKY STUF

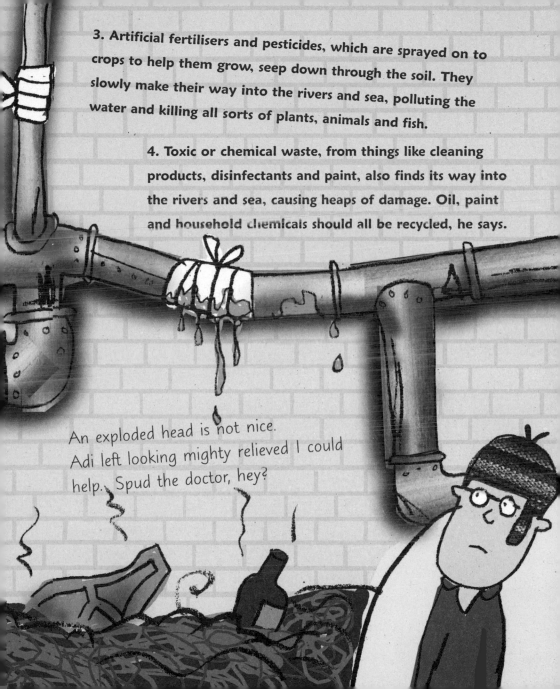

3. Artificial fertilisers and pesticides, which are sprayed on to crops to help them grow, seep down through the soil. They slowly make their way into the rivers and sea, polluting the water and killing all sorts of plants, animals and fish.

4. Toxic or chemical waste, from things like cleaning products, disinfectants and paint, also finds its way into the rivers and sea, causing heaps of damage. Oil, paint and household chemicals should all be recycled, he says.

An exploded head is not nice.
Adi left looking mighty relieved I could help. Spud the doctor, hey?

Friday 8th April

Today I'm going to go not just green but 'organic'.

FACT OF THE DAY: Most farmers use artificial fertilisers and pesticides to help their plants grow and stop pests munching on them. But these plant sprays seep into the skins of the fruit and vegetables. Organic food, on the other hand, is grown without chemical sprays. It's practically as clean as a whistle and does no harm to anyone.

Lots of people think Bombardier Beetles are pests, but they inspire me. If they're worried something is going to attack them, they bend over and let rip with a boiling hot, toxic chemical fart spray. If I could do that I would be truly proud.

progress Report

Jan   Dec

I am well into the year now. But am I
well on my way to becoming truly green?
Adi says he thinks I'm doing good.

Some fruit and veg absorb more pesticides into their skins than others. And the all-time biggest culprits are:

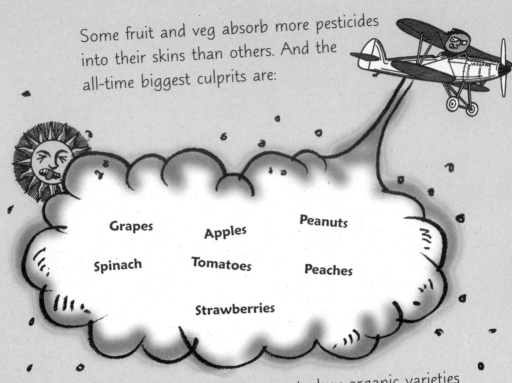

Grapes

Apples

Peanuts

Spinach

Tomatoes

Peaches

Strawberries

So Adi says it makes sense to buy organic varieties if you can or to wash them extra-specially well. He also tells me you can buy organic meat, fish, eggs ... lots of things.

Still no sign of life from my plant pots. I'm having second thoughts. Maybe I did something wrong? Adi says I've just got to be patient.

Monday 11th April

Plants can soak up anything mixed in with the water, not just pesticides, it seems. This morning's experiment proves it.

1. Take a stick of celery and some food colouring.

2. Stir some of the colouring into a glass of water.

3. Stand the celery in the glass and leave it for a few hours.

4. When you slice it up, have a look at what has happened!

My stalk turned as red as a stick of rhubarb! Still tastes good though.

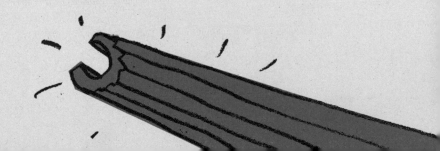

Wednesday 13th April

This morning I found an old wooden box in the shed and got Adi round to have a look. You could tell it hadn't fulfilled its real purpose in life. Could it, like me, go green? Adi thought it could. Which is why it is now .... my Compost Box! Compost contains loads of good stuff, called nutrients, which plants need to grow healthy and strong. We have carried the box over to the house so I can chuck in any of this little lot ...

Egg shells

Fruit scraps, like apple cores

Potato peelings

Vegetable scraps – carrot tops and onion skins, etc.

But no meat. Meat goes smelly, encouraging animals to investigate, and I don't want that. This is important growing compost!

If I throw in the wrong sort of thing that won't decompose, like a crisp packet, it's not the end of the world — I just have to pick it out again a few months later! Very importantly, Adi says, I need to add lots of scrunched-up cardboard or newspaper. Then, when the box is full to the brim, I should leave it to stand for a couple of months.

I have been practising firing stuff into the box from the kitchen window. There are potato peelings and bits of cardboard all over the garden, and a blob of mashed potato has stuck to the windowpane. One banana skin sailed over the fence into Adi's garden.

I watered my pots and trainer, but I'm not feeling very hopeful now that anything will happen. Adi says if he was a seed he'd want a little while to get it together before sprouting. I'm going to give them a bit longer.

Fact for the DAY

There is another way to make compost, without the cardboard, using only vegetable scraps and grass cuttings. In this method the compost pile heats up all by itself – that's the fungi and bacteria eating and reproducing. So if you put a lid on it to keep the heat in you speed up the process. Adi's method makes a little less compost but is a lot less work. Sounds good to me!

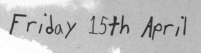

Friday 15th April

Adi came round with an old car tyre this morning. He wanted to recycle it but had run out of ideas. We mulled it over and then had a brainwave. What we need is a swing! I found some rope and the swing is now up and running, or swinging, at the bottom of the garden. We have swung and swung all afternoon.

More news: when I was burrowing under the sink for rope I found two potatoes covered in little white sprouts – they'll be great firing practice for the compost box.

Sunday 17th April

Well, it turns out that not only are those sprouty old potatoes useful for firing practice, they are also good for planting. And April is the perfect time to do it. Adi filled me in on the technique so I got straight to it.

1. I have found a large plant pot at the back of the shed. You could use a bucket but you need to make some holes in the bottom for water to drain out.

2. Make sure your potatoes have grown shoots. If you leave them on a window sill for a few weeks, shoots will appear.

3. Put a layer of compost at the bottom of the pot. 5 cm is about right. Rest the potatoes on top and put in a little more soil to just cover the shoots.

4. Remember to water the pot and when the shoots start showing put a little more compost on top. Adi has been instructing me on this. He's good at instructing.

5. You have to wait now. Every time the shoots grow to the surface cover them over with more soil. Keep doing this until the bucket is full to the brim. This might take a few weeks.

6. When you see the plant flowering you know you're in business.

7. Let the flowers die off, then tip the pot out on the ground, scrabble around and you'll see ... loads of potatoes – and there's no better sight than a muddy spud!

Sim
the
postie →

wednesday 20th April

Sim the postman was waving excitedly
through the kitchen window this morning
and pointing at my plant pots.
Pointing <u>and</u> waving. Something was going on.
I took a closer look. SIGNS OF LIFE!
I take my hat off to Adi: he said it would work.

Sim is a green kind of guy himself and said he was inspired, so I gave him a packet of seeds to get him going.

I have picked out a few shoots from each pot, leaving just the healthiest-looking so that it won't have to fight the others for nutrients in the soil. There's been no sign of life from the trainer. I'm not surprised though. I wouldn't show my face if I lived in a stinky old shoe.

Wednesday 27th April

Plant update: the radishes have shown their faces. It only took a week, but then I have been making sure they are well watered and we've had lots of rain. Adi informs me that the lettuces will take a little longer to surface. Don't they know I want a salad to eat?

Wednesday 4th May

It's getting warm and summery now. I'm spending hours in the garden. This week I'll be planting courgette seeds. You see, I have a plan ...

1. I'm going to plant the seeds in the same way as I did the radishes and lettuces, but when the courgettes grow to about the size of a sausage I'm going to cut my name into the skin of one of them and the name 'Adi' into the other.

2. As they grow the names will grow bigger, but the carved words will heal up and look as though they grew there naturally.

3. Then I'll invite Adi around for lunch and serve him up his personalised courgette. I won't tell him it was me – I'll say the plant taught itself to write. Better get cracking!

I wandered lonely as a cloud...

I've just been talking to Sim and he let slip about a little project he's been working on at home. Something to do with his bike and making delivering the post easier on windy days. But he could tell me 'no more', he said. Top secret stuff.

Friday 6th May

I had a brainwave last night: if it's a good thing to use as little electricity as possible, can I do without electricity altogether? I have a supply of candles for when it gets dark. I can wear extra jumpers if I get cold without the radiators on. I'll eat food that doesn't need heating up or cooking. I'm sure I'll get used to washing in cold water. The tricky thing will be no TV, but I think I can handle that. It's worth a go anyway. All in the name of Greendom.

Things to Remember

1. Adi says that things that get hot, like cookers, use the most energy. If you put lids on your saucepans you can save one third of the electricity you would normally use!

2. Electric kettles get hot so you can tell they use a fair amount of electricity. Which is why you should try to boil only the amount of water you want to drink.

3. Irons use up a lot of electricity so wear clothes that don't need ironing or dress crinkly!

4. Adi says cats watch more TV than dogs, so if I get a pet I should get a dog. He tells me he's done research on the matter.

ooh, it's dark

FACT FOR THE DAY: A lot of electricity is made by burning coal, oil or gas. When they are burned they give off nasty gases including carbon dioxide, which rise upwards and form a layer around the planet, trapping the sun's rays close to the Earth's surface. This is called the 'Greenhouse Effect' because the gases act like the glass in a greenhouse, letting the heat in but not letting it out. The world has warmed up 0.6 degrees in the last 100 years, which might not sound like much, but it is thought to be the cause of floods, droughts and even hurricanes in some parts of the world.

PLANT UPDATE

My trainer is showing signs of life! This blew me away. These plant fellas are tough.

Saturday 7th May

Yesterday's No Electricity Challenge started very well — until the sun went down. I didn't realise I had SEVENTEEN lightbulbs in the house ... till I couldn't turn them on. It was a dark, dark night, and I spent most of it stubbing my toes.

Looking at the mess I made yesterday evening, I have concluded that it is probably going to be impossible and far too dangerous for me to live without electricity altogether. But from now on I'll try to use less instead. Phew, the thought of living like that all the time.

ouch!

Adi says if I want to save energy I should switch off the TV properly instead of leaving it on standby. Or I should buy an electric eel and plug him in.

FACT FOR THE DAY

Eels can produce over 350 volts of electricity each. That's more than most plug sockets. Would the eel like it though?

OFF

ON

Sunday 15th May

Forgot to switch the fridge back on after Friday's No Electricity Challenge. A lot of the food now smells funny, so I've been clearing it out — and in the process discovered a few unrecognisable items that have been in there far too long. I'm going to put it all outside on the lawn for the birds to enjoy.

Adi was full of fridge facts today. Has he been reading up on it? I can't believe he knows all this stuff. He says there are all sorts of things you can do to make sure your fridge uses as little electricity as possible.

1. The back of the fridge should be a little way from the wall to let the air circulate. This makes it more efficient.

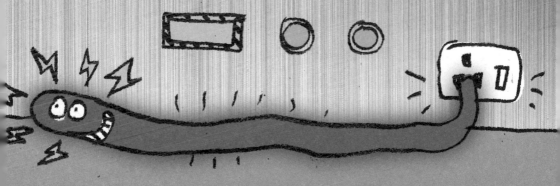

2. A full fridge uses less electricity to stay cool than an empty one. So buy more food! Cool.

3. Fridges use less electricity if they are kept in a cold room like a garage or utility room. This is because they don't have to work so hard to chill the food.

4. I need to remember to keep the fridge door closed!

MY FACT FOR THE DAY:
Fridges use loads more electricity than most household items because they are busy working all year round, day and night, non-stop. A bit like me.

Monday 16th May

The birds — or maybe it was wild animals, or Adi — have been tucking into the contents of the fridge. All that food has vanished! Apart from those few unmentionable items.

I am now enjoying a long glass of cold milk. And it's not from the fridge. How did I make the milk cold? Here's how:

1. I found a clay flowerpot in the shed and brought it indoors.

2. I took a big cooking pan from the cupboard and filled it half full with cold water.

3. I stood a carton of milk in the middle of the pan of water.

4. I turned the clay pot upside down and placed it over the carton so that the rim of the pot was underwater. If you leave it overnight, the water soaks up the sides of the flower pot and evaporates into the air, chilling the pot. Which makes the inside of the pot cold too, and my milk. Magic.

USELESS FACT FOR THE DAY
⬇

Adi says if you farted continuously for seven years you would produce the same energy as an atomic bomb. I think he makes this stuff up.

Friday 3rd June

Adi has been telling me about how important it is to look after the air if you want to be a true greenie. He says everyone should use bikes to get around because they don't produce stinky exhaust fumes like cars. He's got a special bike. It's to build up his muscles. He has to pedal twice as fast as most people to go the same distance and to make it harder work again he drags a stone on a piece of rope behind him. He did a demonstration and was out of breath by the time he got to my house — and he only lives next door.

Sunday 5th June

Summer is here to stay: it looks like it's going to be a hot one! I have decided today's the day that I reuse one of those plastic bottles saved for recycling ... I'm going to rig up a special contraption to have a hot shower without using ANY electricity at all. This has never been done before so it might not work — but I'm an intrepid greenie living in dangerous times ... Adi is taking an interest, but he's going to wait for me to fine-tune the design before he builds one himself.

Try this out:

1. Take a big plastic bottle from your recycling box.

2. Paint it black and leave it to dry.

3. Fill it up with water and leave it in the sun for a day. Solar power will heat it up!

4. Pour it on your head. (The sunnier the day, the hotter the shower.)

PLANT UPDATE
Spud's potato shoots have grown to the surface again so he has covered them up again. Gotta keep 'em working ...

Well, the plan wasn't totally successful. In the rush to try it out I forgot to let the paint dry. I'm blacker now than before my shower. Adi was very excited though. He says this is only the first trial of a very important invention. You can't expect to get things right first time, I suppose.

PLANT UPDATE

The radishes are no more.
They met their end in a very tasty salad.
Think I will plant some carrots next. My lettuces
are growing well. Something has been nibbling at
the outer leaves but I can pull those off quite
easily and eat the rest. I think it might have
been slugs – I'll check with Adi.

Monday 6th June

This morning I saw quite a sight whistling down the road. It was Sim, delivering letters as usual, but with a huge sail attached to his bike. Crazy guy. But very green — using wind power! This was his top-secret project then. I was going to ask if I could have a go, but he seemed to be having problems with the steering and, after pulling him out of the hedge, I thought I'd let him work on the design a bit first.

Adi knows a lot about slugs. He says he keeps a couple as pets on a lead. He had some good ideas for getting them to stop munching my salad too.

1. If you go out on a warm, damp night with a torch, this is when the slugs all come up and start eating. You can collect them up and take them to a bit of wasteland.

2. Slugs like all things wet, so if you make a dry barrier around your plants they won't like crossing it. You can use sawdust, sand, nut shells – lots of things!

3. Slugs love beer – so make a beer trap. Sink a yoghurt tub or something similar into the ground and pour in some beer. In the morning you might find a few dead slugs. Poor slugs.

4. Lots of wildlife eat slugs so make the garden a good home for birds, hedgehogs, toads and frogs.

Important! Whatever you do don't use slug pellets. They kill slugs, to be sure, but they also kill birds, hedgehogs and even dogs if they eat too many.

Monday 13th June

Compost update: it needs help! And apparently worms are the men for the job. Unlike slugs, these little fellas are good friends to gardeners. I'm a big fan, and not only because they are brilliantly wiggly and feel funny in your hand. They eat soil, which is also pretty clever, and their poo is of such superior quality and texture, it's perfect for growing plants and veg.

Monday 4th July

Adi and I fancy a greenie makeover, so we're going to dye some clothes today. Adi says you can use natural dyes and has experimented with grass, mud and berries. And flowers and bark and Ribena. And tea and peas. And mashed pumpkin. But we're going for groovy grass green today:

1. First you have to make a special mix that will allow the clothes to soak up the dye. So find a big pan and put it on the cooker. Make sure someone large and sensible is around to help you.

2. Pour in four litres of water and one litre of vinegar.

3. Drop in the T-shirt, put on the pan lid, turn up the heat and let the T-shirt simmer for about an hour.

4. Then let it all cool down and pour away the mix. (Get the large sensible person back for this. And don't let them do it when it's hot in case they spill some on you.)

5. Rinse the T-shirt in some fresh water. It is now ready for dyeing!

While our clothes were drying we tried to work out what would happen if you took one eyeball out and made it look at the other. Would your brain get confused and implode? I'm really not sure.

This is what you do to dye a white T-shirt green (Adi's most successful product recommendation):

1. Pick handfuls of grass.

2. Mix the grass with water. Add more grass if you want a dark green T-shirt and less if you fancy a light green one.

3. Simmer on the cooker for an hour, making sure the lid is on! (You need the sensible person back again to supervise.)

4. Strain it all. (Sensible person with strong arms.) And throw the grass in your compost box.

5. Dunk in the T-shirt and swoosh it around.

6. Take it out after a few minutes and hang it up to dry.

7. Wear it!

SSSWWOOOOSH

PLANT UPDATE

My tomato plants need more room so I'm going to put them into larger pots. As Sim observed, the one in my trainer looks surprisingly happy so I will leave it there for the time being. I also covered up the potato shoots again today. It turns out Sim did plant up those seeds – and his are sprouting too!

MY BIR

Thursday 7th July

A VERY important day today and one of the finest days of the year. My birthday! Wahey! Adi has just brought me round a great present: a green rucksack. I thought I could take it with me when I go shopping and use it instead of plastic bags, which get thrown away. Adi likes the idea. He says he can now tell that I've got the right stuff to become truly green. I've just got to keep going.

plant UPDATE

My courgette plant is growing beautifully and one baby courgette is big enough to write on. I have changed my mind and written **HELLO** on one and **ADI** on the other. This will be a giggle ...

THDAY

FACT for the DAY

It's a sad fact. Many animals, including thousands of birds, seals and dolphins, die every year because they get caught up in plastic bags that have been chucked away.

friday 8th July

My rucksack is going to be the talk of the town. I paraded up and down the high street yesterday with it loaded up with shopping. I also made an interesting discovery: 'Fair Trade' produce. A shopkeeper had to explain.

1. When you buy something that is labelled 'Fair Trade' this means that the farmer has been given a fair deal and has been paid the right amount of money for it – so he or she should make enough money to live on.

2. It also means that the workers on that farm do not have to work ridiculously long hours or in dangerous conditions.

oops... think I'm on the wrong page!

3. The rules that have to be followed to use the label 'Fair Trade' also encourage organic farming. This is especially important in countries that have not yet banned those pesticides that are banned in other parts of the world. If they are banned in one country it is because they are considered too dangerous to be used safely, in which case they should be banned everywhere.

Today I also discovered that frogs plop into the pond whenever they hear someone coming. I'm thinking of hiding out in the trees so that I can observe their habits and practise burping.

Saturday 9th July

A blue tit has settled in the bird hotel! He looks very comfortable in there. I have called him Bernard. He's been looking at me as I write this, and chirping away. Must know I'm talking about him. I wonder what he's thinking. Can he tell I'm a greenie?

Thursday 4th August

Today I have completely transformed a corner of the garden. It's become a perfect safe haven for wildlife, animals and birds. If they've lost their homes to make way for motorways and houses, they can now come and live over here.

1. The first thing I did was to lay down a few rotten logs and bits of wood for the woodlice. These guys are actually related to seaside crabs so you can see why they like damp places. Centipedes and millipedes will like it here too. Adi says there are more insects in one square mile of rural land than there are humans on the entire earth – that's a lot of little fellas to make homes for!

2. **Next I dug up some large stones for beetles to hide under. Apparently one in four of all the animals in the world is a beetle!**

3. **Next spring I'll plant some flower seeds for the bees and butterflies to enjoy. Adi tells me bees need to flap their wings 250 times a second to fly, so they'll need a rest by the time they get here.**

Army of Frogs

Cloud of Gnats

Parliament of Owls

here, here
order

Clutter of Starlings

what a mess

Colony of Ants

4. I've stacked up a pile of branches and twigs for hedgehogs to hide in if they feel like it.

I'm hoping that soon foxes and badgers will realise my garden is The Place To Be as well. Looking at this patch of garden I'm starting to wish I were a member of the wildlife gang.

Knot of Toads

Charm of Finches

well hello!

Skunk of Foxes

Charge!

Gaggle of Greenies

YAK YAK YAK

Tiding of Magpies

Siege of Herons

Tuesday 9th August

I've been sitting in a corner of the shed observing a spider. All morning. It's been really horrible. But fantastic. But horrible. First I watched him weave his web. He really knew what he was doing.

Then he sat there and waited. So I waited too. And he waited some more. So I did too. Then BLAM! A silly fly wasn't looking where he was going and I won't say what's happening now ... but it looks like the spider's not going to be hungry for a while.

Ooh hello

Looking forward to another solar-powered shower this afternoon! Woohoo! Amazing to think this time last year I had no idea I was going to be so green. And look at me now — heading well towards the true pinnacle of greenness.

SPIDER Facts

1. Weight for weight a spider's web is much stronger than steel. And it is more elastic. It is the toughest material known to man. Wow!

2. A spider doesn't munch its way through any flies it catches in its web – instead it injects a poison that breaks down its prey and turns it into a kind of soup. The spider then sucks it all up.

3. The weight of all the insects in the world that get eaten by spiders is more than the weight of the entire human population.

4. If fruit flies visit your compost box, which can be very annoying, just add a spider ... flies are a spider's favourite meal.

I added some old socks of mine to the compost box today. Just to see what would happen. They might make all the difference.

FACT FOR THE DAY

In their lifetime the average human eats eight spiders while they are sleeping.

aaaaaagh!

Thursday 11th August

Adi showed me a trick this morning — how to grow a red daffodil. It will stick out like a sore thumb!

1. Buy a daffodil bulb, the bigger the better, and a large beetroot.

2. This is the clever bit — and a bit tricky — so get someone big to do it for you. Hold the beetroot and cut out a hollow in the middle. Imagine it is an apple and you are cutting the core out.

3. Then push the daffodil bulb into the beetroot.

4. Dig a hole in the ground about 15 cm deep and plant your work of art.

5. Fill around the bulb with soil and stamp it down. Then just you wait and see what happens in the spring!

Adi planted his foot this morning, to see if it would grow any bigger. When I'd finished planting my daffodil I watered the foot and piled on some compost. Lunchtime came and went, and evening rolled on. I admire Adi's determination in such endeavours. This is what being a greenie is all about. When I dug up the foot this evening and measured it, it was exactly the same size as before. We have discussed why it didn't work and decided that perhaps he should concentrate harder next time. And wait longer.

PLANT UPDATE

Three very tempting tomatoes are slowly changing from green to red. I just have to wait until they are completely ripe, and then that's it! But the plant in my trainer looks to be dying off. Wasn't used to the interesting aroma, I expect.

Sunday 4th September

I have survived a very traumatic and dangerous evening — for months I've been collecting cardboard and cartons and boxes (to use in my compost box) and stuffing them in the little room upstairs. This evening catastrophe hit. I opened the door to add another box, the piles began to wobble and a tower of boxes crashed on top of me. There was nothing I could do. It was like an avalanche. I should have squashed them down first. I've got a lot to learn.

I am now on to the next stage of the composting process:

1. Tonight I will be ripping these boxes into pieces about the size of my hand.

2. I'll then scrunch up the pieces into little balls.

3. Then I'll toss the balls downstairs ready for the compost box. They will mix in nicely with the kitchen scraps and aerate it for the worms and other creepy-crawlies. Those fellas will love it in there. And if they love it, they'll stick around and munch on the rubbish, which will turn it into compost that bit quicker.

Monday 5th September

I got up this morning, and was immediately faced with a momentous problem: I was trapped! A huge pile of cardballs at the bottom of the stairs, barricading my way.

At first I thought my house had been invaded by aliens from outer space — then I remembered yesterday's enterprises. I had to swim my way to the kitchen door.

After breakfast, it was back to business, mixing the cardballs in with the compost. Lucky creepy-crawlies, they're going to love this.

Tuesday 13th September

My wild patch must be a tempting hideaway all right — just before it got dark this evening I caught a glimpse of a hedgehog shuffling around. Hedgehogs are fantastic little guys.

1. **The adults grow to about 25 cm long.**

2. **They hibernate from October through to April in piles of twigs and leaves, so you need to watch out that you don't set them alight when you have a winter bonfire.**

3. **They eat slugs, snails and caterpillars, so they will help stop my salad getting nibbled.**

4. **A hedgehog has about 6,000 spikes on its back!**

5. **Hedgehogs know how to swim and can run up vertical walls.**

PLANT UPDATE

I covered the potato shoots yet again and
now the pot is full to the top. All I have to do is
wait for the shoots to reappear and flower.

My apple trees are looking good. But I won't get apples
for a few years. The plants need to grow quite large, and
to be planted out. Then the tree has to 'cross-pollinate'
with another apple tree – the wind and bees help move
pollen from the flowers of one tree into the flowers
of the other. Only then will the trees produce
fruit. It's a complicated process!

Friday 16th September

6 a.m. Brainwave! I now know what I am going to do with all that newspaper I have been saving for recycling — I'm going to make my own new paper instead ...

5 p.m. I have been busy non-stop this afternoon. First I wheelbarrowed all that paper over to Adi's. He's got a blender. Then:

1. We ripped it into shreds, and blended the shreds with water until it turned into a lovely sludgy pulp.

2. In some mixes we added various things to make it smell good. Like dried herbs, toothpaste and cinnamon. I put my foot down to a couple of Adi's suggestions. Like bogeys. We'd need too many.

THIS PAPER YOU'RE TOUCHING RIGHT NOW is recycled – so you're NOT the first person to use it!

And this is vegetable ink!

3. We added some food colouring to a couple of the mixes.

4. Then we found a big tray, two bits of fine wire mesh and some sheets of newspaper that hadn't been ripped up yet. First things to go in the tray are a few ordinary sheets of newspaper.

5. Next a sheet of mesh. Then some of the pulp goes on top.

6. I squidged it to the edges with my hands and then Adi put the other piece of mesh on top. Finally we added more sheets of newspaper.

7. We took it in turns pressing down to soak up the water, changing the newspaper for new sheets when they got too wet.

8. We have to leave it for about 24 hours to dry out (with a couple of sheets of newspaper on top). Then we can use it! All that for one sheet of paper!

FACT FOR THE DAY: The Amazon rainforest produces half of the world's oxygen supply, so people shouldn't keep chopping those trees down!

Some of these sheets of paper smell really strange.
Adi can't stop smiling. Did he put something funny
in some of the pulp mixes?

I ate those three tomatoes today.
They looked so juicy they didn't stand
a chance ...

Sunday 18th September

We've been picking blackberries. Adi knew just the spot. We came up with a rule that for every berry we ate we had to put one in the basket. But then we started playing a game that involved seeing how many we could fit in our mouths at any one time. I won (37) and I put this down to the amount of talking I do, which has enlarged my mouth.

When we got back home we went to see how my compost box was getting on. I wasn't too optimistic as some of Adi's suggestions aren't always spot on. We poked it with a long stick, just to be sure it was safe to get close. Adi suggested we cover our eyes in case of explosion. But when we peeked over the edge of the box I was pleasantly surprised. Lots of lovely compost. No sign of my socks though. They've vanished. Very mysterious.

Wednesday 21st September

I picked my two prize courgettes with the mysterious writing on today and invited Adi around for a bite to eat. He was sitting at the kitchen table talking about something or other and I pretended that I was getting the food ready. Then:

Adi was up on his feet peering over my shoulder, trying to see. I backed away. 'ALIENS, ALIENS, ADI! THE COURGETTE ALIENS! THEY ARE TRYING TO CONTACT YOU ...
WHAT ARE YOU GOING TO DO?'
Adi saw the message and scratched his head and smiled. A very Adi-like thing to do in a time of crisis.

Well and
truly
GOT

Tuesday 27th September

I was adding a bit of my special compost to the potato pot this morning when I came across a piece of blue fabric that had a very familiar smell. My sock! Like an old friend.

It was almost unrecognisable to the untrained eye, but the smell was a dead giveaway. Where's the other one though? Is it lurking somewhere unexpected and will it give someone a nasty surprise?

Adi came over again today but couldn't stay long – he said he was in the middle of a very important acorn-collecting mission. With Adi, sometimes it's best not to ask.

Sunday 2nd October

The herby homemade paper smells really good. So good that I tried eating a couple of corners. Bit chewy. Too chewy in fact, but the herby one was the tastiest of the lot and it did get me thinking ... I'm going to grow some herbs. I've saved some milk cartons and this is what is happening:

1. I have cut the cartons down with scissors to make them a bit shorter. (DANGER! Watch out for those scissors.)

2. At the bottom I've made a hole with a pencil so the water can drain away. All is going to plan.

3. Now I'm putting in some of my very own compost. Mmmm, lovely stuff.

4. Next, in go the seeds. I've got basil, thyme, parsley and dill. I've put a few in each pot and covered them over with soil.

The seeds are best left inside on a window sill, where it is light and not as chilly as in the garden. I just have to remember to water them.

Adi tells me he's been planting as well — all those acorns. They're baby oak trees in disguise ...

FACT FOR THE DAY: Adi says seeds don't last forever and that it's best to use them within a year. (Another fact: he has to stop eating so many apples. I can't plant the pips fast enough.)

ooh, target practice!

Friday 7th October

At last, my potato pot is ready! The big clue is that the flowers are dying off. I got Adi to give me a hand lifting the pot over to the edge of the garden. We tipped the soil out and ran our hands through it. And there they were: loads of potatoes! I'll be eating them for supper all week. That's another one of Adi's suggestions working out well. I should listen to him more really.

Leaves are falling all over the garden. I've been collecting huge bundles and have made a pile under the swinging tyre. If I'm careful I can launch myself off the tyre, into the air and down to a very soft landing. Excellent fun, but it takes skill, dedication and nerves of steel. You have to time it carefully. If you go too far you end up in the pond. And I speak from experience.

All my clothes are now on the washing line.

Thursday 13th October

I spent today turning the far corner of the garden into a mini-meadow. And the reason why? Well, Adi tells me a meadow is much more interesting than a lawn. It's a place where nature has been left to do its own thing. Wild flowers and grass can flourish naturally and they provide a perfect home for all sorts of animals and insects.

1. The first thing I did was to plant some bulbs from the garden centre. You have to dig down a little way and put the bulb in sitting upright. A good rule of thumb is that the hole should be twice the depth of the bulb.

2. Once the bulb is in and looking happy then fill in the hole and stamp on it to squash the soil down and make the bulbs feel snug.

3. Next spring I will plant some wild flowers. It is a good idea to leave a patch of bare soil around the plants so that they don't have to compete with the grass for the goodness in the soil.

4. I have also bought some wild grass seeds so I'll be planting them next year as well. We'll see what happens.

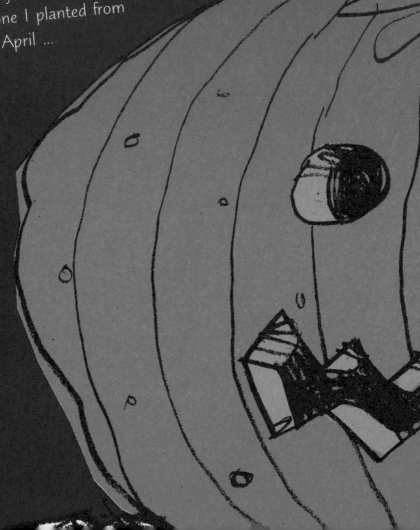

Monday 31st October
Halloween!

I've put a pumpkin by the door with a candle inside.
But not any old pumpkin –
this was one I planted from
a seed in April ...

And how did I do it?

1. I planted the seeds, like the apple pips, just below the surface of a pot of compost.

2. Then the all-important water.

3. When a few tiny leaves appeared I planted it out in the garden and watched it grow. And wow, did it grow!

4. I cut the top off yesterday and hollowed it out with a spoon ready for the candle.

5. Then I cut a face in the skin.

6. Lastly I put a candle inside and put the top back on. I'll light the candle when it gets dark.

I modelled the face on Adi. So, not surprisingly, it looks a bit funny. Adi says he has never seen a more handsome pumpkin in his life.

SPUD'S EXTRA-SPECIAL PUMPKIN SOUP

1. Peel and slice a couple of onions. Get a big person to use the sharp knife and do all the next few tricky bits.

2. Scoop out the inside of the pumpkin and chop it into small pieces. Hook out the seeds – these can go in the compost box, or you could save them for next year's planting.

3. Gently fry the onions and pumpkin until they are soft.

4. Pour in a little water and mash it all up with a potato masher.

5. Add a little salt and pepper.

6. Ladle some into a bowl and place on table.

7. Er. Eat ...

Fact! The biggest pumpkin ever was grown in Canada by a man called Herman and weighed 449 kg.

aaaaaaagghh!! That's one big bowl of soup!

Wednesday 2nd November

If you collected all the world's pee for a day, it would take twenty minutes to flow over Niagara Falls. Why do I tell you this? Well, the doorbell rang first thing this morning, and there was Adi, holding a brick. He rushed straight past me, brick in hand, and disappeared into the bathroom. When he came out the brick was gone. But he couldn't stop to explain - he had to go round and about distributing more bricks. I have hunted round the bathroom but can't see the brick anywhere.

Well. Adi's just been round, and he's explained what he's been doing all day ...

1. At the back of the loo is the 'cistern'. This holds the water that flushes into the loo and then down the drain with all the rest of the muck and bullets.

2. Adi took the lid off the cistern ... and showed me where he had put the mystery brick. Inside! So each time I flush the loo I will save one brick's worth of water. Over time I will save thousands of bricks' worth of water. Enough to build a house. Out of water.

FACT FOR THE DAY: One third of all the water we use is flushed down the toilet. What a waste of good quality drinking water! Go green and pee in the garden (it's very good for compost heaps ...) or buy an environmentally friendly toilet, which has two buttons for flushing so you can choose how much water you use.

Thursday 10th November

Adi won't come outside today because he says it's too windy, so he's standing inside watching my demonstration through the kitchen window. It will show that wind can be a good thing. I have made a windmill out of a cornflakes packet. Here's how ...

1. Take a clean unfolded piece of cardboard from the re-cycling box and cut it into a square.

2. Fold it diagonally from one corner to the opposite corner. Open it out again and fold it diagonally between the other two corners.

3. Cut along the folds but stop 2 cm from the centre.

4. Punch a hole through the centre of the cardboard and one through the same side of each triangle.

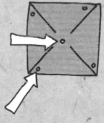
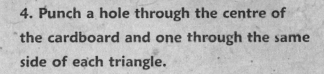

(Get someone big to help with the tricky stuff and scissor action.)

5. Stick a thin straw through the centre hole and bend the corner of each triangle into the middle, pushing the straw through each of the holes.

6. Stick tape over the end of the straw so the cardboard will stay put. And stick tape around the back as well. Make sure some of the tape sticks to the card as well as the straw.

7. Slide the thin straw into a thicker straw so that you can hold on to it. Take it outside and see if it spins!

8. I've tested mine and it works so I've stuck some thread on to the windmill and made a little hook out of a paper clip and tied this to the end of the thread.

My little windmill is spinning madly. Adi is looking puzzled. He doesn't seem to be impressed. But now for stage two! I just have to hook something on to the paperclip ... and here it goes! My windmill can lift a twig. Just shows how powerful the wind can be. If this windmill was much, much bigger it could pump water or make electricity — it would be a brilliant source of energy, and one that would never run out!

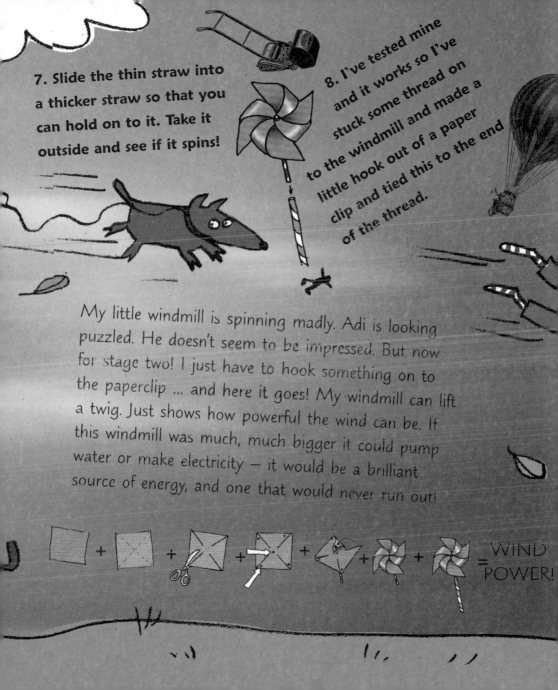

WIND POWER!

TECHNICAL FACT NO 1. Thousands of windmills are used nowadays to make electricity. They are called 'wind turbines' and produce no pollution at all.

TECHNICAL FACT NO 2. Most big wind turbines that generate electricity have three blades. Two bladed models go faster but make more noise.

TECHNICAL FACT NO 3. If you harnessed Adi and me to a turbine and fed us baked beans all day we'd generate a fair amount of wind power too. Why hasn't anyone thought of doing that?

small fart-powered city

Monday 12th December

I have just had a bath and am wondering what to do with all this bath water. Another experiment? I could just pull the plug, but so much effort has been put into making the water clean in the first place. A cunning plan is forming ...

1. I'm going to throw in a load of dirty clothes and stomp about on them. I won't have to use the washing machine, so will save electricity AND water.

2. Once I have stomped about and swooshed the clothes around I can rinse them ...

3. I'll hang them on a washing line in the garden. (No need to waste electricity tumble-drying them when the wind is free!)

Adi offered to help with the stomping in the bath but I know what his feet are like. I politely declined.

Tuesday 13th December

I am about to have an Experimental Shower — with the plug in the bath. Ready, steady, blast!

Well, I'm now clean, which makes a change. But that's not the only important observation I have to make. The bath didn't fill up nearly as much as it does when I have a bath. So Spud, the Great Green Experimenter, can conclude that: showers are the greener way forward — because they use so much less water. Even greener still would be not to wash at all. That is probably taking it to extremes though.

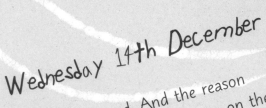

Wednesday 14th December

Covered in mud. And the reason why? .... I had another go on the tyre swing today and timed my launch to perfection. It was beautiful. I flew gracefully through the air and landed slap-bang in the middle of that pile of leaves. Except those leaves seem to be turning into compost.

Adi has just told me this is normal and that people call rotting leaves 'leaf mould'. Mould eats away at the leaves — whereas in my compost box it is the bugs that do all the work.

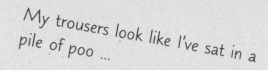

My trousers look like I've sat in a pile of poo ...

Adi says leaf mould can be used to start seeds growing but you should mix it with some normal soil and a little sand for bigger plants.

Saturday 17th December

I cleaned all the windows today with a special environmentally friendly concoction. Adi revealed the secret, chemical-free mix and I have to say — it works splendiferously. No smeary old windows on my house. I don't need to turn on the lights so early in the evening now, which means I am also saving electricity. Don't want to get carried away with this cleaning lark though.

THE PERFECT
WINDOW-CLEANING CONCOCTION

1. Buy a bottle of white vinegar next time you are out and about.

2. Fill a little pot with the vinegar. You could use a small yoghurt pot or an egg-cup.

3. Pour this into a larger bowl and pour in three of those little pots full of water.

4. Mix it up and there we are: a chemical-free window cleaner.

5. Dip a rag in the mix and give a dirty window a bit of a scrub.

6. Then scrunch up a sheet of newspaper and scrub the window again. This will soak up the mix and leave the window gleaming.

Tuesday 20th December

Every morning Adi has a pot of yoghurt for breakfast so ... I thought I would make him gallons of the stuff for Christmas! Lucky Adi. I have just been tasting it for quality control purposes and note: I'm a gifted chef. Mmmmm. It's almost too good to hand over. Just as well Christmas is round the corner or Adi wouldn't even get to see his present.

Anyway, this is how I did it:

1. I heated up some milk in a saucepan, just until it was warm, not too hot.

2. Then I poured the warm milk into a bowl and plopped in a little tub of 'natural live yoghurt'.

3. Next thing was to cover it up with a tea towel and keep it warm under my jumper. Adi told me I looked pregnant. But he couldn't guess what was going on. Ha!

4. All it then needs is to be left overnight to transform into a big tub of yoghurt.

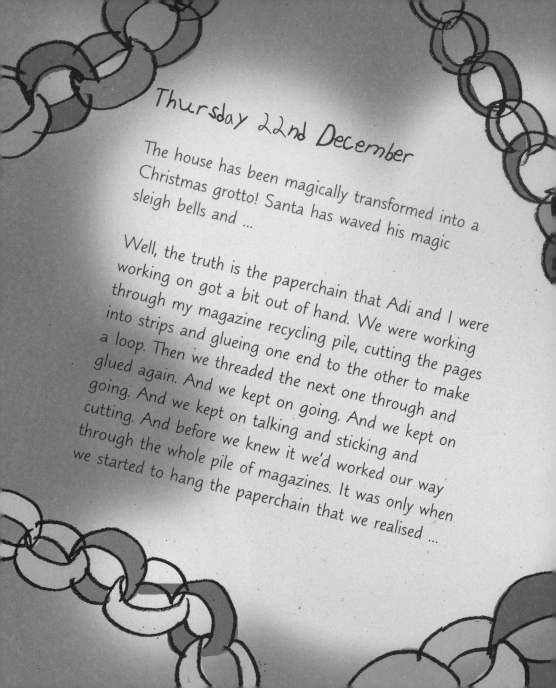

Thursday 22nd December

The house has been magically transformed into a Christmas grotto! Santa has waved his magic sleigh bells and ...

Well, the truth is the paperchain that Adi and I were working on got a bit out of hand. We were working through my magazine recycling pile, cutting the pages into strips and glueing one end to the other to make a loop. Then we threaded the next one through and glued again. And we kept on going. And we kept on going. And we kept on talking and sticking and cutting. And before we knew it we'd worked our way through the whole pile of magazines. It was only when we started to hang the paperchain that we realised ...

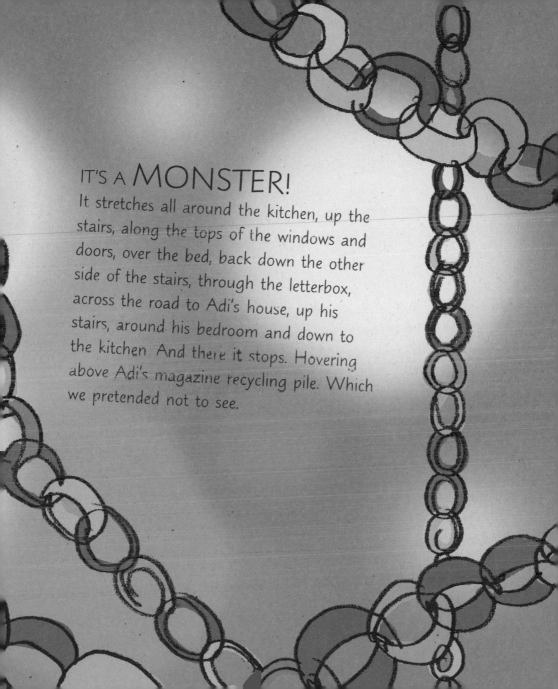

IT'S A MONSTER!

It stretches all around the kitchen, up the stairs, along the tops of the windows and doors, over the bed, back down the other side of the stairs, through the letterbox, across the road to Adi's house, up his stairs, around his bedroom and down to the kitchen And there it stops. Hovering above Adi's magazine recycling pile. Which we pretended not to see.

CHRISTMAS EVE

(and getting excited!)

Yep, Christmas Eve! Tomorrow is the big day, and a big sad day for all those Christmas trees that get cut down. This year Adi brought round a tree that was growing in a pot with all its roots intact. Hooray! We've been adding some homemade decorations. Some look better than others.

Today I've also learned:

Many garden centres dig up trees a few weeks before the big day and cut the roots to fit the pot. This is very hard on the tree. It will probably die as quickly as a tree left with no roots at all. So be sure to buy Christmas trees that are 'pot-grown', not just trees in pots.

Then, to help the tree survive:

1. Keep it in the coolest part of the house.

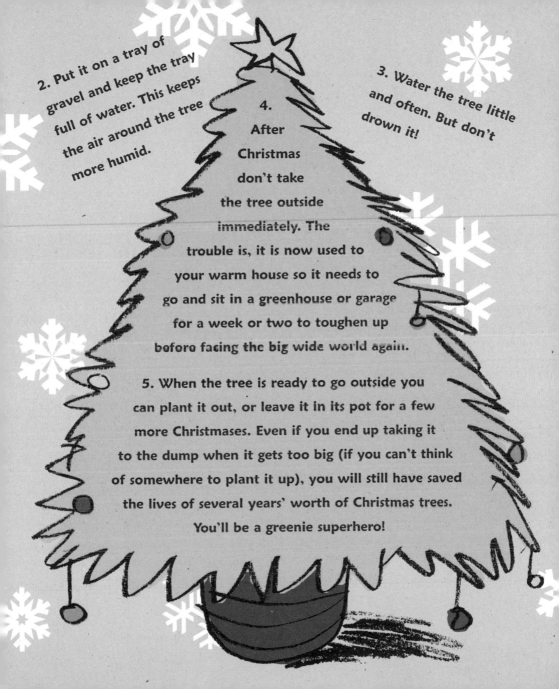

2. Put it on a tray of gravel and keep the tray full of water. This keeps the air around the tree more humid.

3. Water the tree little and often. But don't drown it!

4. After Christmas don't take the tree outside immediately. The trouble is, it is now used to your warm house so it needs to go and sit in a greenhouse or garage for a week or two to toughen up before facing the big wide world again.

5. When the tree is ready to go outside you can plant it out, or leave it in its pot for a few more Christmases. Even if you end up taking it to the dump when it gets too big (if you can't think of somewhere to plant it up), you will still have saved the lives of several years' worth of Christmas trees. You'll be a greenie superhero!

CHRIS DA

I woke up extra early this morning and raced round to Adi's to give him his huge bowl of yoghurt. On the way back I noticed I had left a dribble of yoghurt all the way across the garden and up to Adi's back door. Hope the birds like it too.

TMAS

Adi was delighted with his breakfast and tucked in straight away. I was dead impressed with the mess he made.

Adi gave me a GREAT present: an amazing
multicoloured kite he made himself. And this is how:

**1. Save a bit of soft plastic
from being thrown away. A
black bin bag is perfect. This
is a greenie recycled kite.**

2. Cut it to this shape:

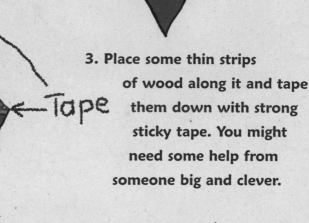

Wooden
Struts

←—Tape

**3. Place some thin strips
of wood along it and tape
them down with strong
sticky tape. You might
need some help from
someone big and clever.**

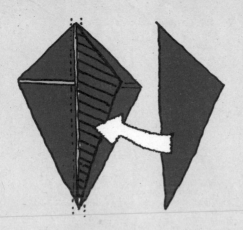

4. Cut another triangle of plastic and tape it along the long middle strip of wood.

5. Reinforce this area with tape and get that big clever person to punch a hole through for the string.

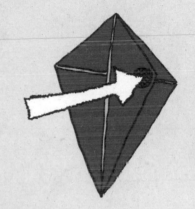

6. You can add a long ribbon for a tail and stick on bits of paper and coloured plastic. These look great when it's flying.

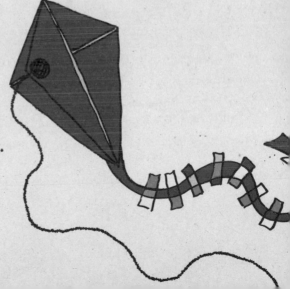

We ate an enormous Christmas lunch — roast potatoes, carrots and onions (from the garden) and an organic turkey. Then a special Christmas pudding — some of those blackberries we picked found their way in there. Yum. We had to provide our own bangs for the homemade crackers. Adi provided burping noises too. Interestingly my burping technique has got quite a lot better thanks to those frogs. I think Adi was taken aback by my progress.

Then, after lunch, we went outside to test the kite. Adi has made a corker! It flew up and up, right over the treetops. We had to keep adding on bits of extra string, even our shoelaces.

Saturday 31st December

One whole year of greenification later and I'm
delighted to declare myself a full-blown greenie! I
know I had a few upsets along the way, but now
I'm practically a pro. This afternoon I set off on a
walk around the garden and admired some of my
efforts: the vegetable patch and wildlife corner,
the bird table and hotel, my beautiful pond,
the mini meadow ...

After a jump on the tyre swing, a big bite of compost-grown carrot and a good swing back and forth, I can safely say I'm feeling very green these days. Yup, truly very green!

The End